Jim Brathwaite

A PROFILE

by Verna Wilkins
illustrated by Dave Thomson

Tamarind Ltd

Oᴛʜᴇʀ ʙᴏᴏᴋs ɪɴ ᴛʜᴇ

Black Profiles Series

Bᴇɴᴊᴀᴍɪɴ Zᴇᴘʜᴀɴɪᴀʜ
Dʀ Sᴀᴍᴀɴᴛʜᴀ Tʀᴏss
Lᴏʀᴅ Jᴏʜɴ Tᴀʏʟᴏʀ ᴏꜰ Wᴀʀᴡɪᴄᴋ
Mᴀʟᴏʀɪᴇ Bʟᴀᴄᴋᴍᴀɴ
Bᴀʀᴏɴᴇss Sᴄᴏᴛʟᴀɴᴅ ᴏꜰ Asᴛʜᴀʟ

Many thanks to Sola Coard for her help on this book.

Published by Tamarind Ltd 2000
PO Box 52, Northwood
Middlesex HA6 1UN, UK

Text © Verna Wilkins
Illustrations © Dave Thomson
Cover illustration © Gillian Hunt
Series editor: Simona Sideri

ISBN 1-870516-47-8

Printed in Singapore

Contents

CHAPTER ONE

Early Years

JAMES EVERETT BRATHWAITE is a successful man, and like so many successful people, Jim says that his success can be traced right back to a teacher at his first school.

This school was Granby Street Junior School in Toxteth, in the middle of Liverpool. Miss Preston was Jim's first teacher. Both she and his parents expected Jim to do well at school.

Just before Jim's sixth birthday, Miss Preston asked her class to write about a walk in the countryside.

"I don't know anything about the countryside, Miss Preston," said Jim.

"Jim, we've been doing a countryside project and we've been reading about it," said his teacher. "You're a bright lad. Get on with it."

"But Miss," said Jim, "I don't know if the pictures I made up in my head are right. I can't write about it."

Later that week, just as he was leaving the classroom to go home, Miss Preston called him back. "James," she said, "I would like you to spend a weekend with me at my house in the country. Would you like that?"

"Oh yes, Miss," he replied, thinking about the wonderful story books she brought from her house

every week to read to the children at the end of the day. He remembered the pictures of her beautiful Siamese kittens, Samson and Delilah. He could have those books and her pets all to himself for a whole weekend!

"Great!" he shouted and flew to the school gate to tell his mother the news.

CHAPTER TWO

Opportunity

HIS MOTHER WAS NOT VERY HAPPY to hear what he had to say. Jim was devastated.

"I thought you'd won a prize or something," she said. "Spending a weekend with your teacher! I'm not so sure. Me and your father will have to talk about that!"

His parents discussed the visit with him, but sent him to bed without an answer. He prayed they would say 'yes'.

The following Monday, Miss Preston gave him a letter to take home. Two days later, his mother and father went to the school. They spoke with Miss Preston for a long, long time.

"Can I go to her house then?" asked Jim.

"Yes son," replied his father. "You can go. Your teacher is a good person. She knows you're a bright lad. She wants to show you the way of life outside this city. We can't do that. You'll be safe."

"And mind your manners," said his mother. "We've taught you how to behave at other people's houses, so don't forget it all."

"I won't Mum," said Jim. "I'll remember to say please and thank you. And I won't burp."

Jim was delighted.

The following Friday, after school, Jim and Miss Preston set off for the country. They drove out of Liverpool, through inner city Toxteth.

From the window of the car, Jim saw the familiar noisy streets, with rows of old cars and battered vans belching smelly fumes into the air. All the houses were squashed together with front doors which opened right onto the crowded pavements.

CHAPTER THREE

A Weekend in the Country

ONCE THEY WERE OUTSIDE THE CITY the
scenery changed completely. Jim sat speechless.

"Are you all right, James?" asked Miss Preston.

Jim nodded and smiled. Then he turned back to
look out of the window once more.

They drove for miles without seeing a single person.
The houses were few and far between. The traffic was
light and the air smelled clean. There were trees
everywhere. The autumn leaves were changing from

green to different shades of gold and brown. On the hillside, Jim could see cows grazing and horses stood tall behind the hedgerows.

"Miss Preston…" he said.

"Yes Jim?"

"I like the countryside."

Just then the car turned into a narrow lane. At the far end, Jim saw Miss Preston's cottage and gasped.

"Wow, and I like your house, Miss. It's not squashed between other houses like at home. And there's Samson and Delilah!"

Miss Preston's cats were sitting on the porch staring at them curiously.

Across the fields, Jim saw tractors, animals and huge barns. "Can we go there?" he asked. "To that farm?"

"Of course we can, Jim," replied Miss Preston. "In fact, why don't we go now. Come on."

It was milking time at Ballards Farm. The farmer squeezed some milk straight out of the cow into a bucket and poured Jim a cupful.

"It's warm!" said Jim, really surprised.

"Yes lad, it comes out like that. The cow didn't heat it up especially for you," the farmer replied, smiling.

Miss Preston was smiling too.

On Saturday morning Jim read seven story books. In the afternoon, he played with Samson and Delilah and Miss Preston read to him. On Sunday, after lunch, they walked by the stream near the cottage.

"What are those Miss?" asked Jim, pointing to some unusual plants growing along the edge of the stream.

"Bulrushes," replied Miss Preston.

"Are those the ones that Moses' mum used to make a

little boat for her baby in the Bible story you read to us at school?"

"Yes, Jim. Well remembered," said Miss Preston. She looked pleased.

Jim had a great weekend.

On Monday morning, Miss Preston's little car queued up in the Toxteth traffic on the way to school.

"Thanks, Miss Preston. I liked being at your house. I like where you live."

"Well James Brathwaite," she replied, "you're a bright lad. All you need to do is work well at school, and you can choose how, and where, you want to live."

CHAPTER FOUR
Origins

JIM WAS BORN IN 1953, more than five thousand kilometres from Miss Preston's cottage in the English countryside

He was born in St Lucy, Barbados, in the West Indies. There, he lived with his mother, father, two older brothers and a baby sister. Although he was named James after his father, everyone called him Ev, short for Everett, his middle name. Jim's father worked as an engineer for an oil company. His mother was a nurse.

Jim's mother was a brave and enterprising woman. She was keen for her family to do well. One day, she spotted an article in a Barbadian newspaper inviting people from the Caribbean to travel to England to work.

These articles appeared month after month in many newspapers all over the Caribbean. They all said the same sort of thing: that England needed people to work as nurses, on the buses and trains and in factories.

"Look, James," Jim's mother said to his father one day. "Read this."

"No, not a good idea," said his father. "I might not get work in England. And I'm not so sure about the weather. That place is cold. Some men I knew who went there came back because they couldn't stand the damp and the forever grey skies. Some of the school teachers who went there to teach weren't allowed to teach. They ended up collecting fares on the buses. It's not for us love."

"I'm sure we can make it, James," his wife continued. "Tell you what, I'll go first and find work and a place to live. You stay behind with the children. Auntie Ianthe will help you look after them. Then, later on, when I'm settled, you can travel with Ev and the little one. The two oldest can stay here at school and come and join us later. What do you say?"

"No!" said Jim's father. "Definitely not."

Jim's mother was determined to travel to England. She saved whatever money she could and borrowed the extra she needed to buy her ticket. She didn't tell anyone what she was doing.

One morning, when the whole family sat together at breakfast, she announced, "I'm going to England."

"What do you mean?" asked her husband.

"Just what I said," she replied.

"When?" asked her aunt in complete shock.

"Today!" she replied. She kissed everybody goodbye and left.

Jim was only two years old and his sister was just a baby when their mother sailed away.

CHAPTER FIVE

Sailing to England

ON A HOT MONDAY IN 1956, just before his third birthday, Jim, his father and his younger sister left Barbados to follow their mother to England.

From the deck of an enormous ship, they waved goodbye to Jim's two older brothers who were staying in Barbados with their grandmother and Aunt Ianthe.

The ship was large and comfortable and Jim's father thought that it was going to be a pleasant voyage. However, when the ship had been sailing for only six hours, he became totally and utterly seasick. He could hardly raise his head.

"What's your mother got us into," he moaned. "And two more weeks to go. Lord have mercy!"

He spent the entire voyage lying in his bunk, groaning. His face sagged and turned a deep shade of grey. The children were worried and upset. They had never seen their father ill.

To make matters worse, the further north the ship sailed, the colder it became. Jim's toes felt numb and sometimes his fingers were frozen. He'd never experienced such cold. His little sister cried and cried.

After fourteen days which seemed like forever, the ship finally docked. With hundreds of other travellers, they walked unsteadily onto firm ground in Southampton, England.

Even though he was only three, Jim would always remember the tremendous shock of arriving in such a strange place. It was so very different from home. The cold, the noise, the hustle and bustle, thousands of suitcases, people everywhere... Caught in the middle of it all, Jim saw only legs and feet and bags, rushing in all directions.

"Now we have to find a train!" moaned his father.

At the station, huge trains screeched and roared and belched smoke like dragons. Jim was both scared and fascinated.

Jim's father, still feeling seasick, with legs like jelly, struggled with a heap of suitcases and the two small children. Eventually they clambered onto one of the trains and set off for London.

"How did your mother manage to write such cheerful letters home?" wondered Jim's father as he sank gratefully into his seat.

Jim and his sister were very excited. They sat with their noses pressed against the window watching the scenery flashing by.

CHAPTER SIX

All Together Again

IN JUST A FEW HOURS they arrived at Waterloo Station, in London, where they were met by relatives who looked after them overnight.

Early the next morning they were ready to travel by train again. This last stage of their long journey from Barbados would take them north, to Liverpool to their mother.

Meeting his mother again was wonderful. Jim hugged her and didn't want to let go. At first, his little sister wouldn't let her mother touch her. She'd quite forgotten her.

Home was an attic room in an old Victorian terraced house in Toxteth, or 'Liverpool 8'. Jim's mother had done her very best but it was crowded. There was a large bed near the window and a small one next to it. A cooker stood in one corner. Three chairs, a stool and a small table were crammed in the middle of the room.

"Where's the rest of the house?" asked Jim.

"This is it Ev, the rest doesn't belong to us. Don't go into the other rooms. Other people live there."

The bathroom and toilet were down two flights of stairs, and they shared it with another family.

"This has to change," said Jim's father, looking around.

Two days later he went out job hunting. He found work as a labourer. No one would give him a job as an engineer. They wouldn't even give him a job at the docks where the men were well paid.

Jim's mother was a trained nurse in Barbados, but she was not given a job as a nurse. Instead she had to work in a factory. It took years and more training, much of which she'd already done in Barbados, for her to get a job as a nurse in England.

CHAPTER SEVEN

Changes

IN 1958, WHEN JIM WAS FIVE YEARS OLD, he started school. He went to Granby Street Junior school in Toxteth. His first teacher was Miss Preston.

Every day, when he came home from school his mother would ask, "How was school today Ev?"

"Oh Mum, call me James or Jim. I get laughed at when my friends hear you calling me Ev or Everick!"

"Nothing's wrong with your name, child!"

"But my name's not *Everick*, anyway! It's Everett!"

"Well, same thing. In Barbados, that's how we say it – Everick. Anyway, it's not as starchy as Everett. It's more loving. Right?"

"Right," sighed Jim, and gave up arguing.

When Jim was eight years old, his father was promoted from his non-skilled job as a labourer, to a semi-skilled job as a boiler man. But the job was in a different town. The family had to move to Warrington.

Jim loved his school in Toxteth. He had some really good friends there. He knew all the children who lived near his house. They all went to Granby Street

Juniors and they played street cricket and football most summer evenings after school and through the holidays.

Jim didn't want to move to Warrington.

CHAPTER EIGHT
House-hunting Horrors

JIM'S MOTHER rang the estate agents in Warrington to try to find a house. Information about dozens of houses was sent to the Brathwaite family to have a look at.

Sometimes, when the family arrived to look at a house they wanted to buy, people would point at them. The owners would say, "Sorry, this house is sold," even though it wasn't.

"Look at this!" Jim's father said to his mother one day, holding up a newspaper. "Where it says 'Houses for Sale' some people have written, 'No Blacks. No Irish. No pets. No children.' This is one strange country!"

The family was worried about where they would live. Finally they found a house they liked and could afford. When they went to have a look at it, a group of neighbours were chatting on the pavement.

One woman glared at Jim and his family and said very loudly, "Black 'uns and all!"

"Why did she say that, Dad?" asked Jim.

"She's saying that the seller shouldn't sell the house to black people. She is rude and prejudiced," his father explained.

"What is prejudiced, Dad?" asked Jim.

"It's an ignorant person who judges people by their skin colour and not by who they really are. It's wrong and she should be ashamed of herself," said his father.

The house felt comfortable and they bought it, but Jim was worried about the neighbours.

"I don't think we should buy this house, Dad," Jim said.

"Why son?" asked his father.

"The neighbours don't like us."

"Well, if we wait for neighbours to like us, we'd be homeless, son. It's their problem if they hate people for no reason whatsoever. We have to get on with our lives."

CHAPTER NINE

Fitting In

IN TOXTETH, a large number of the parents of his schoolmates came from Africa, the Caribbean, Ireland, India and Pakistan. Here, in Warrington, everyone was white. The Warrington accent was different. The games were different. Football was the game in Toxteth and most people supported Liverpool or Everton. In Warrington everyone supported Manchester United, and the school game was rugby.

Fitting in meant changing and Jim wanted to fit in. He began to change his accent. He was a good mimic. At school, he soon spoke the way the other children spoke. At home, he began to try out the Warrington accent on his mother.

"Mam, can I go up pa-ark?"

"What did you say, Everick?"

"Don't call me Everick, Mam."

"Well, don't call me Mam. And don't talk like that," replied his mother.

At home both parents spoke with Barbadian accents. Jim soon learned to switch between Barbadian,

Liverpudlian and Warrington accents comfortably. He remained Everick or Ev at home and became Jimmy at school.

Throughout all this confusion and change, Jim managed to keep his school marks high. His favourite subjects were maths and science. Both parents encouraged him and made sure he did his homework. They were keen for all their children to do well at school. They gave them as much support as they could.

Every day his mother asked, "How was school today, son? Any homework tonight? Everything all right?"

Sometimes Jim walked into the house and before his mother could say a word, he would chant, "School was great. No homework tonight. Everything's all right." And they would both laugh.

CHAPTER TEN

Standing Out

IN 1964, Jim passed his eleven plus examination. This meant that he could go to Grammar School. His parents were delighted, and so was Jim, but he was sad too, because once again his life changed dramatically.

All his friends in the neighbourhood went to the local Secondary Modern or Technical School. Jim's Grammar School uniform was a distinctive blue blazer with a bright yellow badge and he had to wear a cap.

Jim now stood out from all the other children in his neighbourhood. His school was a bus ride away. He had to leave early and he was often late home at the end of the day.

His new school had been founded in the time of Henry VIII, around 1546. The bright shiny badge spelled it out. The Grammar School boys were mostly middle class. Their parents were bank managers, doctors and lawyers. In those days, it was unusual for a working class child to be at a Grammar School. Jim was also the only black boy in the whole school.

It was not easy to find new friends and his old friends called him a snob. Because of his colour, he was easily visible and stood out from the rest of the

boys in the classroom and in the playground.
However, he was totally invisible in all the books and
learning material in the school syllabus. None of the
books they used had any photographs or illustrations
of black people. His new classmates had grown up
with stereotypical ideas of black people and let him
know it.

"Was that your dad, Jim?" they would taunt him if
there was anything bad on the news or in the papers
about a black man.

"Don't be so stupid," Jim would reply. "Do I think that every horrible white man is *your* dad?"

There were times when he was totally miserable. He was picked on.

Many of the aggressive boys at school often tried to start fights with him. Jim wondered if the only black men they knew anything about were the boxers who appeared on television. He wondered if that made them think that all black men fought for a living.

Finally Jim decided that some of the boys were just horribly aggressive.

He tried to avoid the trouble makers, but it was impossible.

And then, it happened…

CHAPTER ELEVEN
The Big Fight

ONE AFTERNOON, WALKING HOME ALONE from school, Jim heard footsteps and voices behind him. He walked a bit faster and the footsteps behind him quickened too.

As he turned to look back, the two boys following him broke into a run. Jim took off. He galloped along, but his school bag was heavy and they soon caught up with him.

One smashed a fist into his ribs and the other shoved him to the ground. His satchel flew across the road. Jim felt a sudden rush of fear, then extreme anger flashed through him.

He managed to leap to his feet and gave one of the boys a mighty shove. The boy rolled down a slope and went face down into the mud at the bottom.

Jim grabbed the other and shook him, screaming, "Leave me alone, idiot!"

But the boy hit Jim hard on the side of his face. Jim reeled, but regained his balance and went for him.

They fought on the side of the road until Jim gained the upper hand and shoved his attacker down the slope to join his friend in the mud.

Jim grabbed his satchel and ran home.

"Goodness gracious me! What's all this, Everick?" cried his mother as Jim tried to sneak into the house and upstairs without being caught.

His shirt was badly torn, his trousers were filthy and he had a cut lip.

"Been in a fight," he mumbled through his cut lip. "Not my fault though. They're always getting at me," said Jim.

"I'm going straight to the head teacher, right now!" said his mum.

"NO! Please Mum. No, it's all right. They'll leave me alone now."

"I hope you don't get into trouble for this! I still think I should go to the school," argued his mum.

"Please Mum. No. It's all sorted. It won't happen again."

And it didn't. Jim believed that the fight was about dominance, or getting the upper hand. Winning the fight gave him more status than getting straight As in science.

Jim had already won much respect in the school as a brilliant rugby player. A few weeks later, he was made captain and he led his team to victory against the boys who had ganged up on him. At the end of the game, they shook hands. Although they never became real friends, the boys never picked on Jim again.

CHAPTER TWELVE
University

JIM LOVED SCIENCE. In 1970, he took four 'A' levels and passed them all. He was delighted and his mother cooked a fantastic Caribbean feast to celebrate.

"You've done well, Ev," said his father. "Tell me, what do you want to do with your life?"

"I want to be a marine biologist," replied Jim.

"What is that exactly, Ev? I'm not sure I know," said his father.

"That's just what my Careers teacher said, so I've applied to do physiology and zoology at university and then see what happens afterwards!"

In October, 1972, Jim left home and went to Sheffield University to do his degree.

"This is the life," Jim said, as soon as he settled in. "Everyone should do this."

He enjoyed university much more than he had ever enjoyed school. He loved looking after himself and enjoyed his independence. He worked hard and played hard. He made life-long friends. He partied.

He played rugby and squash for the university teams and still supported Manchester United, but his real love was cricket. At every opportunity he went to cricket matches. When a West Indian team visited England, Jim would do his very best to go and watch them play. They were brilliant players and won many games all over the world.

In 1975, Jim graduated from university with an Honours Degree and joined Beechams, a large pharmaceutical company. He moved south to Sussex, to work at their company headquarters. He worked successfully in the Accounts Department and then, after two years, he moved to Marketing.

He then applied for a job as head of one of the company's overseas branches. Although he was well qualified for the job, he was told that his colour might be a problem for the locals, so the company didn't appoint him.

Jim was furious at this prejudice. He resigned and moved to another company in the same line of business.

Bayer Pharmaceuticals recognised Jim's talents and, in 1979, when he was twenty-six years old, he was appointed Marketing Manager.

CHAPTER THIRTEEN
Going Solo

AFTER EIGHT YEARS of working for large companies, Jim made a huge decision. He had been thinking for some time that he should set up his own business. He asked a friend to join him. Together, they planned and set up a video company.

On the day the company opened, the two men sat in a small room with one telephone, looking out of the narrow window, onto the street outside.

"What have I done?" Jim muttered. "I've given up a secure job, big salary, company car, and now..."

It took a couple of years, and the support of the bank manager who believed in Jim, before the company started to grow. It was the success of that company that eventually earned Jim millions of pounds. When he bought his own beautiful home in the countryside, not too far from the sea, he remembered Miss Preston and her beautiful cottage by the stream.

Running his own company was difficult and stressful at times. He had many employees who

depended on him for their monthly wages in order to take care of their families. Jim took this responsibility seriously and worked extremely hard. He relaxed by listening to his favourite rhythm and blues tapes and going to cricket matches whenever he could.

One series of matches he would never forget was the one in 1984, nicknamed the Blackwash because the West Indian team won every single match. Jim took his father and business friends who were interested in cricket to the Oval cricket ground in London for the final match of the series.

Together with thousands of other West Indian supporters they arrived at the Oval. Some fans brought music. The team included magnificently talented players such as Malcolm Marshall and Michael Holding and the supporters saw some world class cricket that day.

When any of the West Indian bowlers raced down the pitch, legs flying, arm held high, the crowd tensed. You could hear a pin drop. And when the ball thwacked a wicket or a well-padded leg, the crowd went wild. The fans burst into wild clapping, singing and cheering.

The excitement went on and on throughout the series. The visiting West Indian team beat England in every single match – something that had never been done before, or since.

"It was electrifying," Jim recalls with glee, even fifteen years later.

CHAPTER FOURTEEN

The Benefits of Success

JAMES EVERETT BRATHWAITE IS A BUSY MAN. He owns and runs five companies. He is involved in many others, ranging from electronics to film, television and computers. He travels all over the world.

Although he has done exceptionally well, he still has other ambitions. He aims to own a television station, because he would like to give black producers the chance to achieve success in the film world.

"I enjoy making it happen for others, especially when they deserve it and have not been given a fair chance," says Jim. "The more I do, the more I can share."

His work takes up most of his week, but he likes relaxing at weekends with his family, watching Manchester United football team play and eating his favourite Caribbean dish of peas and rice.

Sometimes he and his family spend their holidays on the beautiful beach near St Lucy in Barbados where Jim was born. He loves to play cricket on the beach with his children, thousands of kilometres away from the hard grind of running his businesses.

Here are some of Jim's thoughts on life.

I look forward to each day knowing that I will learn something new. The older I get, the brighter I get because I'm always learning.

Remember:
It's cool to be smart.

Learn about life, about people, about opportunities.

Everyone has a chance to better themselves.

If you can't become successful working for someone else, then work for yourself.

Enjoy your work – I do – and... it's better being rich than poor!